Things Like This

Dave Alcock

Logo by Morgan G Robles
mxmorgan.com

Editor: Jennifer L. Martindale

Arroyo Seco Press

www.arroyosecopress.org

Cover picture: Dave Alcock

ISBN: 979-8-9895659-5-5

For my family

Forever — is composed of Nows

Emily Dickinson

Contents

Fall

I remember the sparks of the bonfire, which scattered through darkness like schools of small fish. And I remember the flowing scarves of flame, which heated our chests through our damp plastic coats. I remember those dahlias in the sky. Our brightening faces. The glittering petals. And later, the shivering fingers, the match and the matchbox as we huddled beside the wood. The burning fuse that raced like a raindrop to the box of danger that I held in my hand. The smiting flash. The light-speed excision. I remember the cast. I remember laughing at my stump. It's funny. There's so much I remember. But your words of guidance I seem always to forget.

That Boy

Matthieu has stolen someone's lunch and crouches in the shadows beside the steps that lead to the main doors on the western side of the cathedral. It is afternoon. Wintertime. The plane trees whistle in the distance. Their branches are skeletal and dark.

Matthieu puts the baguette to his mouth and takes another savage bite. "How could that boy be so stupid?" he thinks. "To handle what he owns so carelessly. I barely stole this. Just picked it up, from his hands."

Gaps

It wasn't the mizzle that frightened him as he picked his way down to the cove, nor the gale force winds, nor the tide height, nor the surging sea that splashed grey to the cliffs. It was that thing in the gaps beneath his footholds, that scratched and darted between driftwood and rock, which he told himself could have been an otter, but which he knew deep down was a rat.

Sun Squares

It was almost noon on a Wednesday morning in July, and the year's final weekly meeting of the village toddler group had just taken place in the Parish Hall. John Litttlechild, and a handful of other parents from the group's organising committee, had just finished packing away and tidying up. The toys and climbing frames had been stacked neatly in the shed, the plastic plates and cups washed up and stored. John had swept and wiped clean the floor and now, since the others had said their goodbyes and left, it was his job to lock up the doors.

With his youngest son Blake trailing along at his side, John double-checked the fire-escape and unhooked the main swing doors, but as he stopped at the doorway and put his hand in his pocket for the key, he turned around and looked back into the hall.

During the summertime, in the morning, when the weather is good, the sun streams down on the Parish Hall's east-facing wall, and through each of that wall's three sash windows it throws a sloping column of light. On the dark wooden floorboards, it casts three slanting yellow rectangles. At first, they are long and reach out almost to the stage at the front of the hall, but as the sun rises and moves west, these bright squares of sunlight shorten and change direction, until they strain towards the swing doors at the back.

John stood still in the doorway. His eyes settled on the sun squares, and for a moment he considered their change of direction and shape. "How strange," he thought. "For four years I've been coming here, and never before have I noticed them change." Then he looked up at the windows and remembered something he'd forgotten to do. "I must just close the curtains," he said to Blake. "I'll do *this,* then we'll both go outside."

He walked over to the east-facing wall and pulled two sets of curtains shut. Two of the sun squares vanished, but, at the third window, John looked up and stopped. Through the glass, he saw the small, grassed garden, into which the children often went to play. It was there that they splashed in paddling pools or hurtled on ride-ons down the sloping concrete path. There that they chased and tumbled or looked at insects that lived in the ivy on the fence.

As John looked through the window, a look of sadness came slowly to his face. Blake was four. He'd go to the primary school in September. Their time at the toddler group had come to an end.

For a moment, John's eyes closed, and he remembered all the things that had happened in the hall. He saw his children crawling in baby-grows, standing and staggering, then sitting upright on chairs. He recalled helping them to climb up ladders. He heard them giggling as they slipped down slides. He saw them baking things, and making things, and singing and laughing with their peers. He saw them changing their shape and direction. More clearly than ever, he saw his children growing up.

"Growing up?" John wondered incredulously. He went cold with a feeling of loss. "My children have ceased to be toddlers," he thought. "The time of their infancy has come and gone." He looked again through the glass at the garden. His throat tightened and his eyes cooled and blurred. And he hesitated, soft with nostalgia, wishing he could live through that special time again.

Then a voice groaned wearily from the doorway. "Come *on,* Dad! It's time for us to *go*!"

John blinked and swallowed deeply. He took a breath and forced his feelings back down. "You're right," he said, and he drew the final set of curtains, and the last golden sun square disappeared from the floor. He turned around and went quickly through the darkness. And he said, "It's about time we locked up the door."

Mortician

What he
was doing
was embalming

himself.

Not his body
—that would perish—
but something

else.

With only words,
he put spice
on his

perceptions,

his visions,
his glories,
his frights.

It

was his soul
he tightly
bound with

metaphor,

That it might die,
then unbound rise
in others'

minds.

Submersion

Billy looked out of the window as his father drove him to school. It was November and it was raining, and although it was morning the day hadn't come. Cones of streetlight still stood on the pavement; they put little flames in Billy's wide shining eyes.

"Dad," he began. "Why is it that adults don't cry very much?"

Billy's father laughed. He considered, then he sighed. "Because adults learn to hide their feelings. We keep our emotions hidden. It's called self-control."

Billy leant to one side and looked over his father's shoulder. The tail-lights of the car in front of them brought a fiery blush to his small round face. He looked at the other lane of the carriageway and saw the sharp headlights of an approaching car. He saw the hazy white columns beneath them, that went straight through the glistening black roughness of the road.

"You'll learn this too, Billy," continued his father. "As you get older, you'll *learn* not to cry." The rain pattered on the roof and windows, and then his father's voice grew deep and sad. "You'll learn how to bury your fears and sorrows. You'll know how to hide them in your own secret place. Your face won't show pain. Your eyes won't shed tears. You'll learn to pretend that your feelings don't exist."

Billy looked down at a puddle that was spreading inwards towards the crown of the road. He heard the wipers swinging back and forth rhythmically, felt the rumble of a bus, heard water crash beneath its wheels. He looked through the windscreen, at two straits of dark water that were getting deeper on his left and his right. And he imagined he was escaping on a disappearing causeway, racing against the waters of an incoming tide.

Congeners

One of them is lying in the dust close to the fence. The others are facing her. Her eyes are half closed. She looks tired, breathing deeply. The plumes of her chest go up and down. *Why is she looking away?* I wonder. *Why has she turned her back?* One of the others comes forward, reptilian legs stalking, thick-boned toes stretching, claws pointed as murderers' knives. She advances so slowly and still the one in the dust looks away. The stalker lowers her shoulders, clucks quietly, indifferently, and pecks. It is a hard peck. An attack. I recoil. And the one in the dust merely blinks. This goes on and, because of the cruelty, I turn away. But I go back. Now those blinking eyes are closed, and the dead feathers are pale with the dirt. And the stalker is squawking excitedly, and the other ones are gathering around. Maybe they're taking turns now. But the big one is still in charge. The pecking is now a feeding. Each blow is a ravening bite. Until the stalker takes hold with her beak and begins tugging and ripping from the body, then noisily flapping her wings and rising up in flight with the dead one's springing, uncoiling intestine dangling pinkly and wetly from her mouth. And in the air now there is not just this horror, the savage congener and the other-worldly entrails, there is my innocence and my feeling of safety, my childhood trapped as it ceases to exist.

Conspirators

"Why not?" she demanded. "Why *can't* I say things like that?"

"Because things like *that* are hurtful," he insisted. "Things like *that* should never be said."

From outside there came the rumble of a bus. The engine hummed and faded away. And from the distance came the revving of a motorbike. The exhaust pipe cracked. The engine growled and died.

"But I was only saying what I felt. I was telling the truth. What's wrong with that?"

Her father looked out at the garden and saw the poplar moving about in the wind. He watched the branches swaying back and forth slowly, and the silver undersides of the flapping green leaves. "We can't always tell the truth." He shrugged. "Some things we have to keep to ourselves."

The girl shook her head and squinted. "So I can think things, but not say them out loud?"

"Sometimes we have to say nothing. Sometimes we have to say something else."

"Something else?" she cried bitterly. "Are you telling me I have to learn how to lie?"

His eyes were veiled and reluctant, but gently he nodded his head.

A draft slipped in through the window, and the curtains rose up into the room. Outside, the poplar whisked again, and an aerial creaked beside a chimney as it shook.

Seed

Spokes blur. Tyres thrum. A boy circles his back garden on his bike. His father crouches in frozen horror. A nestling mouths a silent scream where it lies. Its eyes flame. Agony blossoms. Its wings stretch and are still at its sides. Clouds move and over-shadow the garden. A floating seed goes dark in the shade. The father turns. His son still circles. A bladed thought cuts a slice through his mind.

Ice

"So have you met anyone yet?"

For a moment Pete looked uneasy. "No," he said. "But I don't really want to. I'm happy as I am. Emma and I still go on holiday together. I still get to see the kids."

Jon nodded. The wipers rasped in front of them and cleared a sheet of slush that had built up on the windscreen. Jon leaned to one side and squinted at the line of tail-lights on the road up ahead. "Must be settling on top of the hill," he said. "Guess they've had to close the road." He reached for a knob on the control panel. "I'll put on the heating. We could be here for a while."

A stream of hot air poured out of the vents on either side of the dashboard. Jon put his hands out to warm them and felt the comfort pool around his wet and tingling feet. "I saw her," he said. "Emma. The other night."

"Oh yeah?" said Pete. "Whereabouts?"

"We were in that pizza place, down at the quay."

"I know the one. We used to go there a lot. The place with the ice cream. The kids love that ice cream. Is that why she was there? Was she there with the kids?"

"No," said Jon. "She was with someone else."

Pete blinked uncertainly. "Sally, was it?"

"No. It was no-one I knew."

"Must have been someone from the netball team."

"No, Pete. She was there with another man."

Pete didn't move, but slowly his eyes darkened with disappointment. Then he turned and put his face to the window. He stared sullenly at the blackness beside the road.

Jon looked at him and sighed. "They were holding hands all night, Pete. Kim said she saw them kiss. She looked happy. She looked really happy. I'm sorry. Emma's moved on."

Pete kept staring through the window. Jon turned and looked straight ahead. He gazed vacantly at the beams of his headlights and watched the flakes of ice falling slowly through the night.

Dreams

Returning, she pulls me from sleep. Opens my eyes. Makes me crawl across a bed. Gives me a torch. Has me shine it beneath a dresser. Reveals a snake and an unsuspecting frog. Enacts a hunt. Shows a strike. A gruesome ending. Then twists. Sinks her teeth into my neck.

Hand

When Ben Challis was nine years old, he watched a scout scoop a ten-ounce harbour crab from the marsh with his hand. Frightened he'd get pinched, the scout not only *scooped* the crab out of the water, but in the same continuing movement, *catapulted* it with as much strength as he could muster, several metres into the air.

The crab followed a flight path that took it all the way from its life-long home in a creek on the marsh edge, through a short sweep of thin blue sky, to its final destination and its sudden violent death on the impacted mud of the quayside car park.

The incident left Ben horrified; filled him with pity and fear and disgust. The murder was shocking and inescapable—it was completely unpoetic and unjust.

Shortly afterwards, Ben's crabbing days came to an end. He grew up and he grew old. But throughout that time, he never forgot the crab. He tolerated it at the bottom, in the darkest grooves of his mind. And he always refused to think about it when, on occasion, it came to the top.

Then, after an interval of many years (which seemed to Ben to have been no time at all) he woke up one morning and was terrified to see the hand of the scout. It approached him from his blind side and slipped beneath his bed, then it waited to launch him skyward, on a one-way journey from the world.

Vanity

Clarke parked the bin trolley on the promenade and took a seat next to Richard on the bench. He gazed up at the sky and smiled. "Looks like spring is here at last," he said.

Richard smiled back at him, then turned to look again out to sea. The grey clouds of the morning were shrinking. Shafts of yellow light were descending from the sky. Spots of sunshine glittered on the water and the white waves crashed and foamed where they broke on the shore.

"You local?" asked Clarke.

"No. Visiting. I have a day off work," replied Richard.

Clarke nodded slowly. "What do you do?"

"I'm a teacher."

Clarke nodded again. "Do you enjoy it?"

"No," said Richard. He closed his eyes and felt the sun warming his forehead. His neck and ears went cool as they were brushed by the wind. "But it keeps me in touch with literature. That's what I teach."

Clarke fell silent for a moment. "Li-te-ra-ture," he said at last. "What's that?"

"It's writing about life." Richard's eyes opened and he spoke sleepily. "It's about things we know but keep on forgetting. It's writing that surprises us by telling us about ourselves."

Another breeze sprang up and slipped over the grey and purple pebbles of the beach. A leaf of brown sea lettuce flapped and a shred of dry bladderwrack rattled. The washed-up disc of a beer can lifted and knelled on the hard round stones.

Clarke turned his body toward Richard and leaned his shoulder against the back of the bench. His left leg straightened in front of him. His heel touched the ground. His toe cap pointed straight up. "Which writer do you like the most?" he asked.

Richard shrugged. He looked at the light on the water and considered. "Shakespeare," he said vaguely. "Thomas Hardy. John Steinbeck." He shook his head.

Clarke nodded. "And have you ever tried to write better than them?"

At first Richard frowned. Then he thought about it. He opened his mouth and was about to speak, then he stopped and thought about it again. Slowly, a glimmer of possibility entered his eyes. "No," he said quietly. "I haven't. Now that I think of it, I've never really tried."

Clarke smiled warmly. "That's it then. Maybe that's what you should do."

Clarke stood up and took a step across the promenade. He stretched out his arms, took a breath, then turned round. "I think it's important that we all have heroes," he said. "But I think we should remember that, like us, they're just people." He took his trolley and rolled it away down the promenade, and the white gulls made circles in the blue sky above his head.

Richard blinked and looked out at the sea. He pulled a notebook from his jacket pocket. He saw the dark buoys on the silvery water and a pair of seabirds that were skimming across the sea. His eyes awoke to the blaze of the horizon. His pen found the paper and words followed it across the page.

Collision

"It has to move the reader," insisted Larry. "The sentiment at the story's end is what the reader will take away." Then he turned — as the taxi pulled out, crossing the path of an oncoming truck—and saw his doom sliding slowly towards him, feeling not pathos but amazed disbelief.

Inheritance

Charles was standing on one side of the car park, pointing at something in the sky. Next to him was his four-year-old son and next to his son was his seven-year-old daughter. All of them were looking up.

The morning sun had risen over the crown of the dry green oak tree that swung its loosening acorns over the far end of the car park. Wide rays of warm, honey-coloured light glanced over its glowing crest, then streaked down onto the line-marked tarmac. Brown dust stood out thickly on the unwiped back windows of parked cars, and wing mirrors and headlights reflected dazzling white stars.

The sky was blue and cloudless, and up where Charles was pointing could be seen the crisp white semicircle of the Moon. "What we can see is the Moon's eastern side," Charles said. "The Sun is coming around the Earth and shining on one side of the Moon. But the Earth is casting a shadow, which covers the bit of the Moon we can't see."

Charles looked down at his children and saw that his explanation had left them behind. He scowled and shook his head. Then his hands opened and came out in front of him. His knees bent a little, and as he moved between the children, his whole body seemed to quicken with life. "Look," he said, suddenly making a fist of his left hand and holding it out between the boy and the girl. "Imagine this is the Earth." He paused, and his right hand came up, and began moving in circles around the fist. "This is the Moon." He looked around, searching for something, and his eyes fell on his son's shock of soft blonde hair. "You're the sun!" he said.

The boy shrugged shyly and giggled.

Charles's fist came back up amongst them. The Moon started spinning slowly around it, and when it reached its far side, it stopped. "The Sun is shining on the Earth—" Charles swung his head towards the boy, and this time both of the children laughed. Then he waited a moment, and when he spoke again, his words came slowly and softly through silence.

"The Sun is shining on the Earth. It's beaming down on our side of it, right now, like a very powerful torch. Rays of light are lighting up one whole side of our planet, but they're also glancing around the side of it, and passing beyond it, far into space. They're lighting up the sky above us, and they're lighting up the surface of the Moon." He looked up again at the white semicircle, and the children quickly looked up with him. Then he took a quick, deep breath, and his eyes came back to the fist. "But the Earth is casting a shadow, which travels for thousands of miles through space, and that shadow has fallen over half of the Moon's surface. That's why we can't see it. That half is covered by our shade."

Charles stopped speaking. Gradually his body loosened. His knees straightened. His hands came down to his sides and slipped softly into the pockets of his jeans. For a moment, they all stood still and looked curiously at the Moon in the sky.

Then the little girl raised up her fist and began rubbing it on one of its sides. "The Earth is casting a shadow," she said. "*This* part is covered by our shade."

Charles smiled and nodded.

He turned his head and looked beyond the car park into the near distance. He saw the clock on the church, which was shining like gold. Then his hands came out of his pockets, they fell to his sides, and his children took them. And together, they walked out of the car park, along the path, through the fields, to the school.

Out

A room. A chill. A nausea. A void of blackness into which you descend. A separation. Lost faces of loved ones. Your life spins like a penny down a well. A scream recalls the shining wonder above the chasm. Something echoes and you unhold. Your name resounds.

Companions

The door of the regional office opened and Jamie came through it. He walked across the empty car park and stood in front of a line of five tired men. It was late and behind him the sun was setting. The men had to squint when they looked up from the ground.

"Right," Jamie said. He had a broad Norfolk accent. "Let's make this simple." His index finger came up and pointed sharply as he stressed his words. "*I'm* gonna ask some questions, and *you're* gonna give me some answers." He pulled a notebook from his back trouser pocket, opened it, and from its pages took out a pen. "Let's start with you, Gary," he said, "and you, Patrick. What time did you two get picked up this morning?"

"'Bout seven thirty," said Gary vaguely. He looked at Patrick who nodded in agreement. "Seven thirty," Gary said again.

"And what time do you normally get picked up?"

"'Bout six," said Gary. Patrick nodded.

"Do you two normally arrive early?"

"Sometimes."

"So you were probably there for more than an hour an' an 'alf?" Gary and Patrick shrugged. Jamie wrote something down in his book. "And what about you, Paul?" Jamie didn't move or look up, but he raised his voice and cast it further down the line.

"I was there at six fifteen and the bus arrived at seven forty-five."

"That's another two hours then." Jamie scribbled something else. "Andy?" he shouted. "What about you?"

"The bus came at eight. I was there since 'alf six."

"Another two hours," said Jamie quietly, and gravely he shook his head. He finished writing, then closed the book around his pen and replaced it in his back pocket. He hitched the waist of his trousers up over his hips, puffed out his chest, and looked up. "Right," he said. "You four." His finger came up again and sliced through the air in front of the men's faces. "You'll get your pay for today, and you'll get paid two hours extra for the waiting. You're goin' to a different factory tomorra— a brand new assignment in Suffolk. It's further away, and it'll take longer to get there, but at least you've still got your jobs." For a moment his face brightened, then his smile vanished and a look of cruelty filled his eyes. He turned portentously to the fifth man in the line.

The man was old, tall, and slight with stooped shoulders. A tonsure of thinning silver hair stuck out wildly from the sides of his head.

"John. What 'ave you got to say for yourself?"

The old man's hands opened and came up helplessly in front of him. "I didn't mean to turn up late," he whimpered. "My alarm clock didn't go off."

"Oh! Well, that's a shame," said Jamie softly, "because that alarm clock has lost you your job."

The old man's face crumpled and his arms dropped to his sides.

"And I'll tell you something else." Jamie took a step toward him. "Thanks to *you* and your *laziness*, our assignment with the company in Norfolk has been terminated. We're lucky we've still got the contract. So when I pay these people for the time they spent waiting around this morning, I'll be takin' the money from *your* pay packet." The old man's eyes closed again. He groaned and his head fell forward. "You won't be gettin' paid anything for today, John," said Jamie. "And after this, I don't ever want to see you again. Now get lost. You can find your own way 'ome."

The old man looked up. His eyes were startled and his mouth had fallen open. He staggered backward and looked around at the closed office blocks, deserted car parks, and empty roads of the out-of-town business park where they stood. "I can't get 'ome from 'ere!" he said pleadingly. "I live twen'y miles away!"

"You should 'ave thought about that this mornin'," snarled Jamie, "when you decided to stay in bed." He pointed at the road beside them that went up and over a hill behind the office. "Now go on." He moved threateningly toward him. "Fuck off!"

The old man almost tripped as he backed away. Then he turned and started walking, but at the top of the hill beside the office he stopped and looked back. A wind lifted strands of his white hair and they turned gold in the light of the sunset. "I don't even know how to get there from 'ere," he whined. Then he turned and tramped snivelling over the hill.

Jamie turned back to the other temps. He pointed his thumb over his shoulder and shook his head. "Don't worry about 'im," he said. "'E deserved it." Then he smiled. "Now, who's gonna drive the minibus tomorra?"

Limbo

Because your room will never be emptied and the photos will stay on the shelves and my cries at night will keep frightening our neighbours and you'll keep hiding in the corners of my eyes, I'll continue writing on these pieces of paper and sticking them with tape to that post with the flowers, believing you'll find them in that space between carriageways, beside the rushing wheels and the breathtaking speeds.

Evenings

Only after her letterbox eyes, the doorstep kisses and bubbling spaghetti, the bathtub giggles and bedtime stories, did he remember that she still wasn't real.

Transients

As usual, he'd collected her from the station and they were driving through the countryside on their way to the coast.

"I'm leaving," she said.

He glanced at her. "Okay. Let's make the most of today."

He looked through the windscreen at the white van ahead of them and saw the scroll of shadows that raced across the back of it: a telephone mast and a road sign, the gnarled extremities of woodland silhouettes.

When they got there, they walked across the clifftops. They stopped on a headland and looked at the sea. It was blue and the horizon was misted. Rainbows came and went in the spray above the surf. "I wish I could stop the clock," he said. "I wish I could keep this from slipping away." A fulmar soared on an updraught and the song of a skylark bubbled down through the wind.

On their way back, they came to a fieldgate and they leaned against it with their forearms on the bar. The hills rolled and the dark woods bristled. A buzzard circled above a shining green field.

"It's beautiful," she said.

He nodded.

She moved her fingers across the lashes of her eyes.

And later, when they went to the beach, they looked at the waves from the water's edge. They gazed as the ocean rippled, as reams reared, and light-points glittered. They gaped as combers galloped and threw back manes of hissing white mist.

He turned. "And you can't reconsider?"

She looked at the skyline. The decision was made. Then she took his arm and placed her head on his shoulder. The breakers pounded and the world seemed to shake.

Equanimity

Swaying, as the ambulance carves corners, its wheels bruising tracks on the newly gritted roads, his son far away, his heart still pounding, he imagines falling flakes. A white world. A yellow moon.

♦

"Home." His voice is desperate. "Please will you take me?" He won't agree. Won't consent. He knows it's close. That nothing can stop it. The room is a noose. He just wants to run.

♦

There's an envelope on the overbed table. "You can take it. It's signed," he says. At the door, his son looks and pauses. Nods and smiles. Love flames in his eyes.

♦

Before the blooded body, before the rushing of doctors, before all the alarms that blare like World War III, he speaks final words. Gasps quickly, "I'm going under." A hand holds his arm. It is impossible to breathe.

♦

Cul-de-sac. Bungalow. Kitchen. Morning paper delivered. Radio alarm come and gone. On a doily on the worktop, the week's drugs neatly organised. Objects keep sparking with an immortal wish to live.

Father and Sons

Samuel was the oldest and he was in the first year of a doctorate. He seemed always to be in the library around then, so Mark was relieved when it was him who answered the phone. "Hi Sam," he said. "It's Dad."

"Oh, hi, Dad," said Samuel. "How you doing?"

"I'm fine," said Mark. "But I need to talk."

There was a pause. "Oh. Sure. Wait a minute."

Mark heard music and conversation in the background. A lid clashed on a saucepan and a woman laughed, then a door thumped shut and the music and laughter stopped. There were hurrying footsteps on floorboards, then a loud crackling sound, and Samuel's voice came back on the phone. "Okay," he said brightly. "What's up?"

"I have to tell you something," said Mark. "Something you won't want to hear."

"Right," said Samuel.

"Your Mum's here with me now, Sam. She's upset. She's been crying for a while."

"Crying? What's wrong? Dad, is Mum okay?"

"Your Mum's fine, but I've done something I shouldn't have. For three years now, I've been having an affair."

"Oh," said Samuel.

There was a long and bewildered silence.

"Your Mum found out yesterday. It's been difficult, but we wanted you to know. Her name's Stella. You met her last summer. And her son's called Caleb. I named him. He's my son."

Samuel stayed silent.

Mark waited and then he called out. "Sam? Are you there?"

"I'm here," said Samuel at last. But his voice was quiet, as if he'd already moved away.

"Your Mum wants you to come back and see her," blurted Mark. "We both want you to come back home."

"I'll be there," said Samuel faintly. He said goodbye and he put down the phone.

Mark looked down at the receiver. He bowed his head and he covered his eyes. Then he looked up blearily and dialled another number. And he waited to speak to Jonathan, who was another of his sons.

Persephone

Like the snowstorm that blows inside an opal, turned to a liquid and dripping from her hand. She rubs the sheen with the tips of her fingers. Her eyes centre. Her mouth opens. She sees. The bits move. They glide in circles. A ball of colours unfolds on her skin. The rainbow arches. The hues keep descending. The pigments keep streaming through smiling lines in her cheeks.

Strandline

Her feet are sore, but she won't say this. The ground she walks on subsides, the soil is sandy and the tufts of grass, nibbled scarce by rabbits and hares, are spongy. But she's relieved to have come off the shingle. It seemed to be refusing. To be draining her of strength. She watches her youngest son in front of her as he swings towards the rattling scrub and, beyond that, to the bony little house. She sees the marshes and the water and the coastline. She decides that this is where they'll stop for a rest. Her shoulders are burning. She knows this. But she does not know how badly. She doesn't foresee the blisters that she'll discover the next day and the tormented pink skin that will look like it's been flayed by fire. They find a nice place to sit. The boy lies down as they talk. So honestly, as if nothing is hidden. He closes his eyes, and she sees the wreck of a scuttled boat. Metal corroded. Off balance. Windows kicked in. She wonders what it would be like to rub her fingers round the rusted sides of one of the holes in its hull. How the edges would cut her, their oxides dissolve, whirl dizzying through storming blood in her veins. She imagines the distance between this place and home — her husband, the boy's father, their marriage. The boy is sleeping. Utterly untroubled. The distance is a blanket that protects him from hard rain.

Sycorax

"I'm a witch," she said, and you thought *How ridiculous!* Though, even then, you felt something like fright. She was crazy, but she was also magnificent. Your mentor at a school. Perhaps the best you would get. Brawls fizzled out as she glanced down corridors. Silence fell as she swept into rooms. You locked your door. She left hers open. But her desk was perfect. No-one touched it. No-one dared. The dysregulated purred as she charmed growth from them. Hackney's wildest lapped *sententiae* from her hand. Cerise hair and blue morpho eyelids. Crooked yellow teeth. A monster. A disgrace. But a progenitor. A maker. A mistress. With an Axl Rose boyfriend who was less than half her age. Such incandescence. Such prominence. Such intransigence. Such vulnerability. Such womanly strength. "I'm a witch," she said. And was it really so ridiculous? Were you not chained by her refusal to comply? Does she not haunt you (years after she has vanished)? Are you not still whipped by the lightning of her eyes?

Want

For the errand that brings us together. For the history that must have come before. For this small corridor and its unexpected privacy. For the half-darkness that holds us in its arms. For our proximity as we meet beside the fire-door. For the wanted notice that I see in your eyes. For the wall behind us that catches our shoulders. For our bending knees that let us slide to the floor. For our lips' impatience and our tongues' authority. For the rushing knowledge that everything has changed. For our perception of our actions' rightness. For our escape from refusal and thought. For my hand's freedom and your knees' separation. I thank you for all of this and I gratefully accept.

Incidents

May was turning left off the ring road when she heard something crash into the nearside of the car. She turned off the engine and looked in the wing mirror. There was a man who'd fallen from his bike onto the road. He brushed himself off and propped his bike up against the railing. He came to face May. His face was bright red.

"What were you doing?" he shouted. "You almost killed me."

May said, "I'm sorry. I didn't know you were *there*."

"Well, you should have done. You should pay more attention."

"But I indicated. Did you try to undertake?"

The cyclist glowered. "I think you're dangerous." He reached into the car and pulled out May's keys. Then he hurled them over the fence of a garden centre. They landed in a pond full of algae and reeds. "Dangerous," said the cyclist bitterly. He mounted his bike and pedalled away.

May got out of the car and looked at the pond through the wires of the fence. Then she turned. The traffic queued behind her. An engine revved and a motor horn beeped.

Edgeland

Sometimes he would be there in the morning and he would look down at the lights of the pit. He would think about his father and his brother and he would wonder what it was that they were doing. Were they digging? Were they drilling? Were they drinking from their flasks of tea? Today the pit was gone, but every now and then he looked down at the valley. There were roads there now and streetlights that led to a car park and some out-of-town shops. But the memories kept coming in flakes, like the skin of his mouth after drinking boiling water, their bladed edges scraping burns on his tongue, their thinning strength breaking up between his teeth.

Reversals

Will had been talking about Valerie when he'd paused and looked at the tealight on the table. Dan had sat still and said nothing. It had been obvious that Will had more to say.

"It's been difficult for her," Will continued.

"Working full-time?" asked Dan.

Will nodded. He peered at the bubbles in his pint of lager, which streamed up to the white collar at the top of his glass. "Val's not a careerist. But when the kids arrived, she was earning twice as much as me. She knew her employer wouldn't allow her to go part-time, so we decided that I'd do the childcare and she'd do the paid work." His eyes closed and his face tightened with regret. "But she would have loved to do the stay-at-home parenting. I often feel guilty that she didn't get the chance."

Dan looked at Will's face over the table. He saw the candlelight on his cheeks and on the soft skin of his protruding lower lip. He watched it flicker on the septum of his nose and on the wrinkles that had piled up beneath his eyes. "You shouldn't feel guilty," Dan said. "They're good kids. You've done a good job."

Will smiled sadly then looked down again at his glass on the table. His eyelids were drooping, but the bright candlelight flickered in his eyes. "I *know* I shouldn't feel guilty, but sometimes I just don't *believe* it. I find myself wishing that I'd been the breadwinner, and that Val had got to stay at home. I keep feeling guilty for all of her sacrifice. I think I'll feel this guilt for the rest of my life."

Sixteenth

He couldn't believe his luck when he discovered that his desk was at the back directly behind Kelly Sylvester's. They had come from different form groups, but somehow had become good friends, and all of that year he sat in his English lessons filled with happiness simply because he was able to look at her. There was so much to notice. The tight curls in her brown and blonde hair. The icy rays in her dazzling blue eyes. The freckles on her cheeks. The white teeth that he spied inside her mouth. She used to turn around and they would talk for what seemed like hours about anything and everything except the books that they were supposed to be studying. Once she was eating an apple and a bead of juice glittered brightly on her lip, swelling with the light from the windows, waiting to burst beneath the tip of her tongue. There were other things too. On one occasion, the teacher asked him what he was reading at home. He told her. "Moravia's *Erotic Tales.*" He saw the aversion of the teacher's eyes, saw them lower with a momentary shyness. He saw the colour that rushed to her cheeks and the hidden smile that gave her lips new shape. Then later, with a different teacher, for a term he studied *Antony and Cleopatra*. One afternoon, they concluded a reading and the question *Is this love or is it lust?* was discussed. "It's both." The boy almost shouted. It was obvious. The two were the same. But the teacher was puzzled by the boy's proposition, as if it were a truth that we know but forget, which sparkles briefly as the juice of an apple, a sweet brilliance that time and age will erase.

Believer

He looked up from the page in the lamplight and peered over the balcony into the darkness downstairs. He waited and he listened. It was silent then he heard it again. Wheezing. Emphysemic. Behind the curtains of the big glass doors.

He got up and moved across the mezzanine. He stood uncertainly at the top of the stairs. Nervously, he descended the staircase. His heart pumped. Blood rushed in his ears.

"Dad?" His voice trembled. A slice of moonlight flickered in his eyes. The breathing sounded. The drapes kept twitching. It seemed impossible. Something was there.

His creativity arose inside him. Reason slept and fantasy surged. He faced the curtains, not knowing but believing, and he waited for a corpse to return from the dead.

Then he remembered: a conversation at the harbour—about the tide—it would rise in the night. He blinked and looked down at his wrist-watch. His eyes closed. His shoulders sagged. He sighed.

The tidehead washed and whispered. The curtains moved around the blowing of the wind. He went up the stairs and sat down at the table. He put down his elbows and rubbed his eyes with his hands.

Experts

The old man stopped and looked out across the field. A butterfly lighted on a wheat stalk and two swallows dived and circled overhead. He squinted and pointed back at the woodland. "I can smell a vixen down there," he said.

"Oh! Can you?" said Will. His voice was interested. "What does a vixen smell like?"

The old man smiled. "Well, it smells like a vixen," he said.

Will nodded and smiled back.

"It's different to a dogfox," the old man explained.

Will kept nodding slowly. Then he paused for a moment. He shook his head. "I wouldn't know the smell of a fox if it was right under my nose," he said sadly.

"Well, you're young," said the old man. A fly buzzed around him and he swept it away with the back of his hand. "And not a lot of people do, even the so-called experts. Even that fella on TV." He shook his head in scorn and laughed. "He's always sticking his nose up at forty-five degrees." Will laughed as the old man looked up, blinked delicately, and twitched his nose. "Hasn't got a clue!" the old man chuckled.

The sun filtered through a gap in the cloud cover and left a patch of brightness on a distant yellow field. "Once he was talking about dry stone walls," the old man went on. "One of them was dry inside and he said that's how they got their name." He scoffed. "It hasn't got anything to do with that, you know. They're called dry stone walls because they're made without mortar!" He laughed merrily. "Hasn't got a clue!"

The butterfly fluttered above the wheat again, and the swallows shrilled happily overhead. In the distance the sheep kept bleating. A jackdaw cawed. Their laughter hovered above the field.

Wishing Well

The memory crept towards him like a plant. The vapourless air engulfed him. The moistureless dust choked him. Then, beneath a roof and a bucket, there billowed the shadow of climbing jasmine on a floor. A stone circlet suddenly widened. A disc of black water came glittering up a shaft. Her blue eyes brightened. Her soft hands coiled. Her white smile sweetened and ripened and swelled. A smell of hot pastry twisted and tightened. Coffee gripped. Wood roasted and cricked. A grain of spice cracked in two like a seedpod. Small stars bloomed and ripped the shell of his heart.

Our Bread

Everything seemed to stop. William's accordion lay silent against his chest and Beatrice stopped giggling. We held the warm slices in our hands and breathed in the sweet smell of sugared dough. Even there, standing on the grate above the sewers—the smell of sugared dough.

And as we put the bread in our mouths, our eyes blinded with contentment, our stomachs grew quiet, and our bodies loosened and became still.

And a woman stared as she stood beside a newsstand. Her eyes were envious behind the veil of her hat. And she was unhappy not to have the things we clung to, the thrill of surviving and the taste of our bread.

Lorikeets

Look up and you may see it. A screen of brightly coloured birds that flushes through the treetops like a psychedelic wind. Here, where the sky is grey and the leaves fall thin and yellow; where wet mud slips beneath a worn-out shoe sole and a toe squeaks inside a water-logged sock. Where a foot aches and a body is powerless; where a neck creaks and stiffens and rebels. Beyond the high-street, beyond the traffic, the pavements. Beyond the markets, the arcades, the stalls. Beyond the people, beyond the gate, beyond the entrance. Beyond the memories. Beyond the grief and despair. Where hope fails and vision is flightless. Look up. Lorikeets may be there. With bibs red as volcanic lava. With faces purple and frosted as plums. With feathered wings green as ripe avocados. Look up. Lorikeets may be there.

Dancefloor

And then, in slow motion, leave the edge and take a place near the centre. Be greeted. Be embraced. Be applauded. Face the waves. Don't retreat. Don't cringe. Strive. Break the bars of refusal. Climb the wall. Blow holes. Take flight. Hear the call. Pulse of drumbeat. Flow of bassline. Tunnel deep. Find the sound. Sail the words. Be a fool. Take a joke. Don't remember. Do what's right. Open up. Let it in. *But what first? Move my arms? Swing my shoulders? Shake my head? Bend my knees? Stamp my feet?* Stop caring. Allow the music to guide you. Be good. Choose a brand-new way. Like falling. Like sliding. Like surrender. Turn the key. Free the stranger within. Now smile. Know that life is this simple. Have fun. Feel your chains disappear.

Things Like This

The shelf in the riverbed was behind them and so was the roar of the rough white water. The river was now almost motionless. It was glassy and gliding and calm. Paul watched a current as it slid round a boulder and marked the river's brim with a spinning silver stream. He saw the mirrored trees going down through the waterway, toward the blue sky beneath a mass of green leaves.

Then his daughter's voice came shrilly from behind him. "What is it?" She pointed at the path. Paul's head swung round from the river. His eyes squinted, came open. He smiled. "It's a shrew," he said amusedly, and all four of them stepped forward to have a look.

The handful of grey fur moved deliberately across the woodland footpath. It hurried past some fallen brown oak leaves and stopped beneath some ferns on the wayside bank. The children squatted in front of it. They watched it clean its fur in the shadows beneath the leaves.

"*I* think it's a vole," whispered Angela.

"Maybe," said Paul. "But I've never seen one as closely as this."

It climbed up the bank in front of them, traversed a ledge, and disappeared down a hole. Paul straightened up and frowned. Slowly, he shook his head. "I saw one once before," he mused. "Many years ago. I spent the whole of one summer looking for it." He paused. "I only ever saw it that once." He turned again from the bank beside the footpath and looked through the trees to the wide brown river. "You can spend the whole of your lifetime looking," he said quietly, "but you won't see anything, unless you get some good luck." His eyes moved over to a sunbeam, which broke on a wind wave into a galaxy of stars.

Then the little boy stood up. He turned and looked searchingly at Paul. "But we *are* lucky, aren't we, Dad? Aren't we lucky? To *see* things like this?"

Paul turned, and his face was in shadow, but the glints sharpened in the sockets of his eyes. A ray of light had pierced the treetop above him and his family were brilliant in a yellow shaft of light. "Yes, we are," he agreed. And he looked altered. Then he took the boy's hand and they set out again along the path.

Acknowledgements

Many thanks to the team at Arroyo Seco Press: my publisher, Thomas R. Thomas, and my editor, Jennifer L. Martindale. Thanks also to the editors of the publications in which the stories of this collection first appeared or were later reprinted: Camille Gooderham Campbell, Michelle Elvy, Tomek Dzido, Simon Webster, Karen Schauber, Keith Hoerner, Lorette C. Luzajic, and Natalie Welsh. I am indebted to all those who have advised and encouraged me during the time it has taken me to write this book and would like to extend special thanks to John Brantingham, Clare MacQueen, and James Thomas, whose guidance has been indispensable. I am, in addition, grateful to those who have organised the flash fiction communities and reading groups within which several of the works included here were developed: Jude Higgins and the team at Bristol Flash Fiction Festival; Nancy Stohlman at FlashNano; Paul Beckman at Flash Bomb New York; Meg Pokrass and Francine Witte at The Prose Garden. Finally, I am grateful to my family, without whom the stories in this volume would never have been written. My wife, Vic; my children, Cathy and Tom; my brother, Ed; my mother, Sheila; and my father – also my first and most trusted reader – Christopher: to you all, my love and thanks.

"Ice" was published in *Every Day Fiction* (December 2017).

"Companions" was published in *STORGY Magazine* (April 2018).

"Vanity" was published in STORGY Magazine (August 2018).

"That Boy" was published in *Flash Fiction Festival Two* (2018).

"Succour" was published in *Every Day Fiction* (December 2018).

"Our Bread" was published in *Flash Fiction Festival Three* (2019).

"Sun Squares" was published in *The Cabinet of Heed* (April 2020).

"Transients" was published in *Flash Frontier* (May 2020).

"Things Like This" was published in *The Cabinet of Heed* (August 2020).

"Inheritance" was published in the *Journal of Radical Wonder* (May 2022).

"Submersion" was published in the *Journal of Radical Wonder* (November 2022).

"Conspirators" was published in the *Journal of Radical Wonder* (November 2022).

"Father and Sons" was published in the *Journal of Radical Wonder* (November 2022).

"Incidents" was published in the *Journal of Radical Wonder* (December 2022).

"Reversals" was published in the *Journal of Radical Wonder* (December 2022).

"Experts" was published in the *Journal of Radical Wonder* (December 2022).

"Seed" was published in *MacQueen's Quinterly* (March 2022).

"Gaps" was published in *MacQueen's Quinterly* (March 2022).

"Fall" was published in *MacQueen's Quinterly* (March 2022).

"Want" was published as "For the Errand that Brings us Together" in *MacQueen's Quinterly* (May 2022).

"Limbo" was published in *MacQueen's Quinterly* (May 2022).

"Congeners" was published in *MacQueen's Quinterly* (May 2022).

"Out" was published in *MacQueen's Quinterly* (August 2022).

"Sixteenth" was published in the *Journal of Radical Wonder* (May 2022).

"Edgeland" was published in the *Journal of Radical Wonder* (May 2022).

"Persephone" was published in the *Journal of Radical Wonder* (May 2022).

"Collision" was published in *The Dribble Drabble Review* (October 2022).

"Equanimity" was published in *MacQueen's Quinterly* (September 2022).

"Hand" was published in *MacQueen's Quinterly* (January 2023).

"Believer" was published in *MacQueen's Quinterly* (January 2023).

"The Mortician" was published in *The Dribble Drabble Review* (January 2023).

"Dancefloor" was published in *Syncopation Literary Journal* (Summer/Autumn 2023)

"Wishing Well" was published in *MacQueen's Quinterly* (May 2023).

"Lorikeets" was published in *MacQueen's Quinterly* (May 2023).

"Sycorax" was published in *MacQueen's Quinterly* (September 2023).

"Evenings" was originally published as "Evening" in Prompts of Resilience (October 2023).

"Strandline" was originally published as "Between This Place and Home" in *Flash Fiction Festival Six* (2023).

"Dreams" was originally published as "Dream" in *Prompts of Resilience* (March 2024) and in *The Dribble Drabble Review* (May 2024).

Biography

Dave Alcock is a writer based in Devon, England. His short forms have appeared in a range of online journals that includes *Every Day Fiction, Flash Frontier, MacQueen's Quinterly, The Journal of Radical Wonder,* and *The Dribble Drabble Review.* His work has been nominated for *Best Microfiction, Best Small Fictions,* and *Best of the Net. Things Like This* is his debut.

Things Like This is a collection shaped by memory, family, change, and the fragile beauty tucked inside ordinary life. These pieces move through grief, childhood, love, aging, and wonder, finding what is tender and unsettling in the everyday. Alcock's language is vivid, lyrical, and sharply observant, rich with image and rhythm. He brings emotional depth to small moments, turning them into scenes that feel immediate, luminous, and quietly lasting. A beautiful read.

—Francine Witte, author of *RADIO WATER*

Dave Alcock's prose poetry is like music propelling you across the dance floor of *Things Like This,* observing with unerring attention the small matters of nature, right at our feet, while keeping an eye out for human misstep and misdirection. These are the same tales told around the dervish bonfire, meditations sung out in Homeric wonderment and disappointment but always in awe. It's impossible not to watch and listen and dance to the stories in this siren song book.

—James Thomas, Co-editor of the Norton *Flash Fiction* anthologies

In his debut collection of flash literature, *Things Like This,* Dave Alcock explores the often-underestimated significance of marginal events. Day to day, we tend to overlook such events as trivial, yet they may shape our lives in unexpected ways. At turns eccentric, uncanny, enigmatic, visceral, and evocative, Alcock's memorable micro-works spotlight liminal spaces and reveal the extraordinary in the ordinary. A marvel.

—Clare MacQueen, editor of *MacQueen's Quinterly*

Dave Alcock's work speaks to me as much as any writer I know and more than most. He writes not so much of the huge life events, but, like a great haiku writer, finds those moments between the moments and investigates them with compassion. I read his work slowly, lingering over the meaning he's drawing from a seemingly innocuous event, then trying to resee it through my own lens. In this, he has me reinvestigating not only my whole life but the way I understand it. These are pieces that will challenge you and help you to grow.

—John Brantingham, author of *Slowly Through the Grove*

www.ingramcontent.com/pod-product-compliance
Lightning Source LLC
LaVergne TN
LVHW011050110826
845149LV00015B/3428

* 9 7 9 8 9 8 9 5 6 5 9 5 5 *